John Scott

Letters to the Right Honourable Henry Dundas

On his Inconsistency as the Minister of India

John Scott

Letters to the Right Honourable Henry Dundas
On his Inconsistency as the Minister of India

ISBN/EAN: 9783744716192

Printed in Europe, USA, Canada, Australia, Japan

Cover: Foto ©Andreas Hilbeck / pixelio.de

More available books at **www.hansebooks.com**

TO THE

RIGHT HONOURABLE

HENRY DUNDAS,

ON HIS

INCONSISTENCY

AS THE

MINISTER OF INDIA.

———————————

LONDON:

PRINTED FOR J. DEBRETT, OPPOSITE BURLINGTON-
HOUSE, PICCADILLY.

1792.

LETTERS, &c.

LETTER I.

SIR,

THE important events which have happened in India in the laft year, naturally excite the public attention, and we may expect that a confiderable portion of the approaching Seffion will be fpent in debates upon the paft and prefent ftate of that country.

A concife and candid examination of the conduct of his Majefty's India Minifters may

be

be of some service to those who neither wish to condemn nor to applaud without a cause. I have imposed this task upon myself, and will endeavour, at least, fairly and honestly to execute it.

I do not impute the part that Mr. Pitt and yourself have taken in the present war, either to avarice, to rapacity, or to a desire of extending the patronage of office ; those who bring such charges against you, act as absurdly and as unjustly towards you, as you have acted in many instances towards Mr. Hastings.

But I affirm it as a fact, capable of clear and incontrovertible proof, and from which, when Mr. Fox brings the subject forward, there can be no defence *in argument*, whatever there may be *in numbers*, that in *the origin of the war*, in *its continuance*, and in *the*

pro-

profeſſed objeƈt to be attained by it, *if complete
ſucceſs* ſhould be the reſult of it, you have
departed *from every principle* that you your-
ſelf laid down, as the *true* and *only principles*,
by which India *ought to be governed*, either
when you were Lord Advocate of Scotland
in the Adminiſtration of Lord North, and
Chairman of the India Committee, as Treaſu-
rer of the Navy under Lord Shelburne, or
as the uncontrouled Miniſter of India, for
the laſt ſeven years under Mr. Pitt's Bill.

I affirm it alſo to be a clear and incontrovertible faƈt, that there is not *a principle*,
which you voted to impeach Mr. Haſtings
for having avowed or aƈted upon, during his
Adminiſtration, that you have not carried
*infinitely beyond what you accuſed him of car-
rying it*, ſince the commencement of the
preſent war.

Three

Three very remarkable inftances have oc-
curred in a fhort period, in which grofs and
wanton injuftice has been feverely punifhed.

The unprovoked and faithlefs conduct of
the late Government of France to Great
Britain during the American war has utterly
deftroyed the Monarchy of that country.

In return for the fupport which Oppofition gave for many years to all the follies and
abfurdities of Mr. Burke, that Senator con-
trived to render the Oppofition unpopular
throughout the country, precifely at the
moment when the Ruffian armament left the
fupporters of Mr. Pitt without an argument
to urge in his behalf, and had even infpired
his opponents with the hopes of overturning
his Adminiftration.

The

The prefent war in India has compelled Mr. Pitt and yourfelf to throw off that mafk of deception which you had affumed, in order to wound Mr. Haftings the deeper, to give *your entire approbation* to meafures infinitely ftronger *than the ftrongeft of thofe*, which were deemed criminal in him to adopt, and to carry your ideas of *conqueft* and extent of *dominion* in India, far beyond any that you accufed him of having entertained.

I propofe, in the courfe of my correfpondence, to take a concife review of the principal meafures of *your adminiftration*; I fay *your adminiftration*, becaufe although his Majefty has appointed fix India Commiffioners, you have been hitherto looked upon as the fole India Minifter, poffeffing the fulleft confidence of Mr. Pitt, who enjoyed, and was, therefore, enabled, to confer upon you the

fulleft

fulleſt confidence of his Sovereign, and both Houſes of Parliament.

It was after a very arduous ſtruggle, with a very powerful party, that you ſucceeded to your miniſterial office, nor did any man, at any period enter into office, under ſo many and ſuch great advantages as you did in Auguſt 1784, when Mr. Pitt's ſyſtem obtained the ſanction of the Legiſlature.

India had been reſtored to univerſal peace, in deſpite of the meaſures which *you* had taken to prevent it, *when no reſponſibility* was annexed to 'your ſituation.

Hoſtilities with the Marattas had actually ceaſed in October 1781, though Mr. Dundas's reſolutions prevented the final ratification of peace with thoſe ſtates until February 1783.

1783. Peace with France was proclaimed in June 1783, and with Tippoo Sultan in March 1784.

Bengal and its dependencies produced an annual revenue of above five millions sterling. Of this revenue and of such resources as could be procured on the Carnatic and at Bombay, you had the entire disposal.

Before I proceed to consider the use which you have made of the resources, *which you have impeached another person for procuring;* it may be useful to trace the steps by which you ascended to your present rank.

The Minister, who had not been able to guard his country from a ruinous war with America, France, Spain, and Holland, thought it very extraordinary that an invasion of the

B   Car-

Carnatic by Hyder Ally Cawn was not prevented, and you were appointed the Chairman of a Committee, inftituted by the Houfe
of Commons, to inquire into the caufe of
that invafion. This naturally led to a review
of the whole political fyftem of India, com-
prehending in it every important act of the
Adminiftration of Mr. Haftings.

After your labours were finifhed, and they
are contained in fix voluminous Reports, you
affected to feel fuch an abhorrence for the
political conduct of Mr. Haftings, that the
very critical and dangerous fituation of India
in 1782, could not induce you to refrain from
moving the moft extraordinary feries of Refolutions (confidering what *you* have *fince*
done *as a Minifter*) that have ever appeared.

I am

I am not of rank enough to fay what the Lord Chancellor did in the laft Seffion, " that " they will remain an eternal monument of " Parliamentary folly and abfurdity ;" but this *I will fay*, that they will remain an eternal monument of the inconfiftency of Mr. Dundas, fince, with complete power delegated to you by the law, *you have, in no one inftance*, adhered to thofe Refolutions ; but, on the contrary, you have *perfifted* in every *fyftem* which thofe Refolutions *condemn*, and have neglected to *redrefs* a fingle grievance, affirmed by thofe Refolutions *to exift*.

The firft important meafure of your Adminiftration, which has been ftrongly condemned, was your arrangement for liquidating the debts of the Nabob of Arcot and the Rajah of Tanjore.

Mr.

Mr. Fox brought this fubject before Parliament, and your conduct was condemned by Mr. Burke in fuch terms, as could not poffibly be ufed with impunity by a Gentleman to a Gentleman, and had never before been applied, even by a difappointed Patriot to a fuccefsful Minifter.

In order to delude *the public* into an opinion that he acted *from conviction*, Mr. Burke, eight months after he abufed you in Parliament, fent his abufe into the world in the form of a pamphlet.

Who that reflects ferioufly upon this circumftance, can in future put the flighteft confidence in the honour of a public man ? Would it have been thought *within poffibility*, a very few years ago, that a difference with his Party, in a matter *which concerns not us,*

fhould

fhould have furnifhed Mr. Burke with a plea for throwing himfelf into the arms of Mr. Pitt and Mr. Dundas ? Or that *they* would have received, with *fo much cordiality*, the man who had held them forth to the world as the moft corrupt and contemptible of human beings, who had folemnly, and in the face of his country declared, " that all the " acts and monuments in the records of *pe-* " *culation, the confolidated corruption of ages,* " the patterns of *exemplary plunder* in the he- " roic times of *Roman iniquity*, never *equalled* " the gigantic corruption of a fingle act" done by yourfelf and Mr. Pitt ? " That in- " cited *by no public advantage*, impelled *by no* " *public neceffity*, in a ftrain *of the moft wan-* " *ton perfidy which has ever ftained the annals* " *of mankind*, you had delivered over to *plun-* " *der, imprifonment, exile*, and *death itfelf*, " the unhappy and deluded fouls, who, un-

" taught

" taught by any former example, were ſtill
" weak enough to put their truſt in Engliſh
'faith ?' "

My reaſon for cloſing my firſt letter with
this quotation is, to impreſs *honeſt men* with
an opinion that no credit ought to be given
to aſſertions, let them come from what
quarter they will, if *unaccompanied by proofs*;
and if Mr. Burke ſhould be *your Advocate*, in
the enſuing Seſſion, which is by no means
improbable, I wiſh to let the public know
what opinion *he* entertained of *your* profli-
gacy, a very ſhort time ago.

ASIATICUS.

Dec. 25, 1791.

LET.

SIR,

AS I have undertaken to point out your *inconfiftencies*, it will be neceffary to fhew in how many inftances you have adopted the plans of Mr. Haftings, *as a Minifter*, and condemned them, *as a Member of Parliament*.

In the latter capacity, you have proclaimed to the world that certain important advantages fecured to this country by the late Governor General, were obtained by exactions, *grinding* and *oppreffive*, by *injuflice*, and by *flagrant breach of faith*.

In

In *your Miniſterial character* you have *annually* taken credit for every increaſe of reſource, *thus fraudulently and ſcandalouſly obtained*, and though enjoined by *a poſitive law* to redreſs *all wrongs*, committed by Britiſh ſubjects in India, you have not *in a ſingle inſtance*, afforded redreſs, thereby holding up the Britiſh Nation to the contempt and deriſion of all Europe.

You have, in fact, followed the example of the Spaniſh Corregidor, who puniſhed a robber for ſtealing a thouſand doubloons, but at the ſame time put the money into his own pocket. I ſtate this on a ſuppoſition that the complaints of wrongs having been done by Mr. Haſtings, are founded in truth. My own opinion is, that the complaints were not well founded; in that caſe, the nation has nothing to anſwer for; but it is impoſſible poffible to reconcile to confiftency, or to any man's fenfe of juftice, the conduct of the Minifter of India.

This will afford an ample field for dif-cuffion to the Hiftorian, the Philofopher, and the Moralift, when the politics and the parties of the prefent day fhall ceafe.

Mr. Fox and yourfelf differed in many points relative to India; but on three very material heads, you were fully agreed fome years ago.

The firft, that the *honour* and *juftice* of this country were concerned, in procuring *redrefs* for all *wrongs* committed by Britifh fubjects in India.

The fecond, that all *offenfive wars*, for the purpofe of *conqueft*, *and extent of dominion*, *fhould be abfolutely prohibited in future.*

C   The

The third, that Mr. Haftings fhould be immediately recalled to Great Britain.

What Mr. Fox *would have done*, I know not, for he loft his office, and failed in his India plan at the fame time.

You have been *above feven* years the Minifter of India—What you have done, *I know*, and in thefe three effential points, you have totally departed from your own profeffions.

When Mr. Pitt's Bill placed complete power, and complete refponfibility in your hands, in Auguft 1784, Mr. Haftings was the Governor General of Bengal—his continuance or his removal abfolutely depended *upon you*—for the veto of the Proprietors had been annulled by the Legiflature.

You

You had moved a feries of Refolutions againft him in 1782, in which all his *political* acts were condemned, commencing with the ftoppage of the King's tribute in 1772, and clofing *with the grant of a fum of money to the Marattas,* and the expulfion of Cheyt Sing, in 1781.

When the Houfe, upon your motion, had voted all thefe Refolutions, you moved, " That Warren Haftings, Efq. having in " fundry inftances acted in a manner repug- " nant to the *honour* and *policy* of this nation, " and thereby brought *great calamities on* " *India,* and *enormous expences* on the Eaft " India Company, it was the *duty* of the " Directors of the faid Company to purfue " all legal and effectual means *to remove him* " *from his office, and to recal him to Great* " *Britain.*"

Prima

Prima facie, we would suppose that a man who would form a pretence to any sort of confistency, would not allow Mr. Haftings to remain for a moment in India, after having given *such a character of him*, and after he not only had the power to remove him, but was deeply refponfible for continuing him in office.

But the whole tranfaction fairly explained, would do you credit, if your fubfequent conduct had not convinced me, that you have never acted upon any fixed principles of juftice, as an India Minifter.

One of the firft acts of your adminiftration was to empower the Directors to tranfmit to Mr. Haftings thofe thanks which his conftituents had voted in the preceding year, and which Lord Sydney had prohibited
them

them from fending to him. Thefe were accompanied by the *unanimous thanks* of the Court of Directors, *with your name figned in approbation, before they were fent;* and to, fhew that it is impoffible to move a ftep without involving you in a frefh inconfif-tency, the thanks were particularly given to him, for his " *uncommon zeal, ability, and* " *exertion in finding refources for fupporting* " *the war in the Carnatic, under fo many and* " *preffing difficulties.*"

Will it be believed, that after *figning your approbation* to this Letter in 1784, you fhould, in thirty months, have voted, as a Member of Parliament, to impeach Mr. Haftings of high crimes and mifdemeanors, *for finding thofe very refources?* yet the fact is literally true.

I

On the 4th of March 1785, you took into confideration an earneft requeft that Mr. Haftings had tranfmitted from Bengal two years before, for an appointment of a fucceffor to his office. It is not poffible for any Minifter to fhew a ftronger fenfe of the merits of a public fervant, than you difplayed in your mode of complying with that requeft.

You begin by ftating, that the appointment of a fucceffor was made, in compliance *with the earneft requeft of Mr. Haftings*. You next acknowledge *his long, faithful, and able fervices*. You fix no particular day for his refignation, but leave it to him to refign the firft convenient opportunity in the enfuing feafon, commencing in October 1785, and ending in March 1786.

Here

Here then was a Governor General, whom in April 1782, you had branded on the Journals of Parliament, " as having in fundry " inſtances acted in a manner repugnant to " the *honour and policy of the nation*, as having " brought *great calamities on India*, and *enor-* " *mous expences on the Eaſt India Company*," continued in office, if he had ſo pleaſed, until the 25th of March 1786, thanked in the *ſtrongeſt poſſible terms* for his ſervices, which are acknowledged to have been *long, faithful,* and *able.*

Such a contradiction could not eſcape the ſagacity of Mr. Fox, and he noticed it in Parliament. Your reply was *bold, manly,* and *juſt* : " That Mr. Haſtings had performed " *great* and *eſſential ſervices*—that he was *the* " *ſaviour of India*—that you *approved* of the " thanks—that he *well merited them*—that it " was true, you had moved the recal of Mr.

" Haſtings

" Haftings in 1782, but now fincerely re-
" joiced that the Proprietors *had refifted your*
" *motion,* as by fo doing, *they had rendered a*
" *very effential fervice to the country.*"

This was faying in effect, though not in
terms, that you had been grofsly miftaken
in 1782. How to reconcile your *fubfequent*
conduct, to this open and manly and *honoura-*
ble avowal of Mr. Haftings's fervices, would
puzzle a whole College of Jefuits.

Mr. Haftings neither accepted the Government up to the period you allowed him
to remain in it, nor waited to receive the
thanks that you tranfmitted to him ; but
peace being univerfally reftored in India,
and Bengal and its Dependencies fixed upon
the fyftem which you have *approved as a*
Minifter, and *condemned* as a Senator, he re-
signed

figned a ftation which he had held for thirteen years; a period remarkable for the
ftruggles of contending factions at home;
for the increafe of taxes, and the addition of
above one hundred millions to the public debt,
for the lofs of empire in America, in Africa,
and in Europe; *and for its extenfion in Afia,*
through the exertions of *that Man,* whom
you have fince brought *to Impeachment.*

On the day of his arrival in London, Mr.
Burke gave notice of his intention to move
an inquiry into his conduct, early in the
following Seffion; and in the fame week,
the Directors, *with your concurrence and ap-*
probation, repeated their *unanimous thanks* to
him for his *long, faithful,* and *able fervices.*

Mr. Haftings well knew that every *mate-*
rial arrangement which he had formed, *had*

D

been

Been highly approved—he knew the great and important fervice that his name had been of, to you and Mr. Pitt, in that ftruggle, which ended in the removal of Mr. Fox—it was natural for him to expect *confiftency* and *juftice* from thofe who fo unequivocally acknowledged his fervices. What then could he fear from a fair inveftigation of his conduct?

Experience muft, however, have convinced him, *that there is no little enemy.* So faid the wife Doctor Franklin, and a wife Italian before him.

When Colonel Popham was encamped in the vicinity of Gualior in 1780, Mr. Haftings defired him always to have in view the capture of that fortrefs. Sir Eyre Coote ridiculed the idea of taking it, without a battering train, and a regular fiege. I met him

him upon the Ganges in July, and he told me, " Haftings muft be mad to think that " the ftrongeft fort in Indoftan can be taken " by two thoufand Sepoys."

Mr. Haftings entertained hopes of fuc-cefs from the confidence which he knew the Marattas had in the natural ftrength of the place ; Colonel Popham efcaladed, and fur-prifed the fortrefs. An action of which you have made very honourable mention in your Reports.

Mr. Haftings in this inftance proved him-felf a very good general for India, but he has been unable to cope with the veteran political commanders of his own country; for, deeply intrenched under your acknowledgement of his *long, faithful and able fervices*, and *ftrongly fortified*, as he conceived, by your adoption

of

of *all his syſtems, foreign* and *domeſtic,* he entertained as little idea of danger from the ſcouting parties of Mr. Burke, as the Marattas from the light infantry of Colonel Popham, when ſheltered by the ſcarped rocks, and lofty ramparts of Gualior.

ASIATICUS,

Dec. 6, 1791,

LET-

LETTER III.

SIR,

As I have not been educated in the fchool of Englifh politics, I will not pronounce that you have acted *uniformly wrong*, becaufe in fome inftances, I cannot reconcile your conduct to any one principle of honour, of honefty, of juftice, or even of common fenfe.

Much that you have *done*, fince you became the India Minifter, entitles you, in my humble opinion, to the approbation of every fair and candid man; but in order to judge impartially of your conduct, I muft ftate the circumftances under which you fucceeded

to

to the management of the Britifh Empire in India.

It had moft unfortunately been the fafhion for fome time prior to that period, to defcribe the countries under our influence, as har-raffed, oppreffed, and totally ruined. You had given into this folly in a certain degree, but the writers of the Select Committee Reports went ftill farther, and Mr. Burke, while the Bills of Mr. Fox and Mr. Pitt were before the Houfe, never fpoke of Bengal, but as of a country ruined beyond the pof-fibility of redemption; we were fuppofed, by him, to have harraffed, and murdered the natives, not by *hundreds,* but by *millions.*

Mr. Francis, who from the rank he had held in India, could neither fpeak, nor write without effect, had faid to the Directors, at

the clofe of 1781, " It is my *moſt ſerious opi-*
" *nion*, that you will *never again* have an in-
" veſtment purchaſed with any ſavings from
" the revenues of Bengal."

Theſe repreſentations always appeared to
me like the ravings of madmen, for I had
croſſed the kingdom of Bengal in almoſt
every direction in the courſe of fifteen years,
and had gone through the province of Benares, and the Vizier's dominions, without
ſeeing any of thoſe marks of miſery and
wretchedneſs, which made ſo conſpicuous a
figure in the Committee Reports; I did,
therefore, venture to ſay, the firſt time I had
the honour to ſpeak in Parliament, that Bengal would yield from the various reſources of
its Government, upon the reſtoration of
peace, a nett ſurplus revenue to Great Britain, of one million, five hundred thouſand
pounds;

pounds; but though you are, as I am, a *sanguine man*, yet you would not, nor would any other Member, *hazard the same opinion at that time.*

I made this calculation upon an idea most undoubtedly that you would very soon discover, *as a Minister*, the follies of your opinions, *as a Member of Parliament*; that you would not be disposed to surrender *a single advantage* that Mr. Hastings had procured; and my idea was a just one.

You have continued the Salt Monopoly, the Opium Monopoly, the Mode of Letting Lands to Farmers, when Zemindars refuse to give the rent that Government demands. You have continued to receive the Additional Revenue from Benares, and the Increased Subsidy from Oude; *and the result is,* that

my

my prediction was much more than verified in *three years*, and the furplus is *now* above *two millions fterling a year.*

The Refolutions of a Houfe of Commons have not the force of law ; but where a Member *moves them*, profeffing too that he means they fhould be as a *warning*, and a *guide*, to an inferior body, one would naturally conclude that he would *himfelf* be influenced by them.

In the year 1782, the Houfe of Commons refolved, *unanimoufly*, upon *your motion*, " That the fimple grounds on which the " Britifh Government ought to have endea- " voured to eftablifh an influence fuperior " to other European Powers, fhould be, the " maintenance of an *inviolable character* for

E " mo

" *moderation, good faith,* and *fcrupulous re-*
" *gard to treaty.*

" That the ftoppage of *the King's tribute,*
" and the fale of *Corah* and *Allahabad* to
" the Vizier, were contrary to *policy* and
" *good faith,* and that fuch *wife* and *practi-*
" *cable* methods fhould be adopted *in future,*
" as may tend to *redeem the national honour,*
" and *recover the attachment and confidence of*
" *the Princes of India.*"

What attention have *you,* as a *Minifter,*
paid to this Refolution, or to any other that
you moved in 1782?

Have you *redeemed* the National Honour,
by paying to the King the arrears of his tribute? Have you paid him one rupee of the
current tribute, to which he was annually
en-

entitled, fince *you* became a Minifter ? On the contrary, you expreffed *a very ferious alarm*, when Mr. Haftings merely exerted his *influence* in favour of the old Monarch.

In what a fuperior light does Mr. Haftings appear to you, in every thing that relates to the Emperor of Indoftan ! !

Mr. Haftings affirmed fairly and openly, in 1773, that by quitting the protection of the Englifh, and ceding Corah and Allahabad to the Marattas, the King had forfeited *his own right* to thofe Provinces, and to his tribute in future. The Provinces he, therefore, fold to Sujah Dowlah, and withheld the payment of the tribute until he received the fentiments of the Directors, who would not ftir a ftep in fuch a bufinefs without the knowledge of the Minifter. Both tranfactions

were

were approved, and Mr. Haftings was ordered
· to difcontinue any farther payment of tribute.

You declared, in 1782, that the conduct of
Mr. Haftings, and of the Company, in this
tranfaction, was contrary to *policy* and *good
faith* ; you farther faid, and fo did Parliament,
that fuch *wife* and *practicable methods* fhould
be taken in future, as *may redeem the national
honour*. If thefe expreffions mean any thing,
they muft mean, that we fhould, at leaft, pay
the King his tribute *in future* ; yet, with more
than two millions a year furplus revenue, you
have not paid him a cowrie: he has been the
fport of fortune, and after having been tortu-
red by a favage, was deprived of his eyes, in
a manner too fhocking to be related.

The man who thinks that we acted towards the King in a manner contrary to *policy*

licy and *good faith*, muſt impute his early miſ-
fortunes to the Company, and to Lord North,
and the more grievous calamities of his later
days to Mr. Dundas. Your opinion and mine,
I fancy, are the ſame, and that you are *now*
as ſenſible, as I always was, of the *impolicy*
and *injuſtice* of thoſe Reſolutions relative to
Shaw Allum.

Mr. Pitt, when he moved his India Bill,
ſeems to have adopted all your ideas—that
treaties ſhould be *inviolably* kept—*offenſive*
wars moſt carefully *avoided*; and to ſhew his
opinion of the exiſting government, he talked
of offences having been committed equally
ſhocking to humanity, oppoſite to *juſtice*, and
contrary to every principle of *religion* or *mo-
rality.*   I

After

After *such a description*, he introduced a clause in his Bill, which ſtates in ſubſtance, " that complaints *have prevailed*, that *divers* " *Rajahs*, &c. &c. &c. *have been unjuſtly de-* " *prived of*, or *compelled to abandon*, or relin- " quiſh their lands, &c. &c. &c. and the " *principles of juſtice, and the honour of the* " *country, require* that ſuch complaints be " *forthwith* inquired into, *fully inveſtigated*, " and, if founded *in truth, effectually re-* " *dreſſed* ;" which redreſs you are, in the ſame clauſe, *enjoined* to give.

This clauſe applies *moſt pointedly* and *di-rectly* to the caſe of Cheyt Sing, many years Rajah and Zemindar of Benares. It could apply to no other perſon under the Bengal Government.

ſ   It

It is perfectly clear, that in 1782, Cheyt Sing was, in your opinion, unjuftly expelled from Benares, becaufe you *reported* his cafe to Parliament, and urged his expulfion as a reafon for the immediate recal of Mr. Haftings; but when you inveftigated his cafe in 1784, you muft *have changed your opinion*, or you would have ordered Cheyt Sing to be *forthwith* reftored, agreeably *to the pofitive injunctions of the Legiflature*. Every rational man muft form this conclufion.

But my underftanding is confounded, as I proceed through the *changes* and *chances* of your public life. For with a pofitive command *forthwith* to reftore Cheyt Sing, if he had been unjuftly expelled, and doing *nothing* for two years and nine months, refpecting that Rajah, I find you, as a Senátor, concurring in proclaiming to the world, " That " War-

" Warren Haftings, in direct breach of his
" duty, *and in pofitive contradiction to the*
" *treaties, ftipulations, and engagements,* which
" fubfifted between the *Eaft India Company*
" and Cheyt Sing, required him to furnifh
" three battalions of Sepoys at his own ex-
" pence, and did extort from him five lacks
" of rupees, under pretence of paying for the
" faid three battalions."

It is beyond my conception how a man, fo
thinking of the demand which led to the expulfion of Cheyt Sing, and who had voted
alfo that " that Prince was wickedly, arbi-
" trarily, and tyrannically expelled from his
" dominions," could fleep a night in his bed
in peace, without doing what the *law* had
pofitively enjoined him to do, namely, to *re-*
ftore him to his dominions.

But

But the farther I advance, the more does my aftonifhment increafe; for you had fcarcely fent Mr. Burke to the Lords with this your *folemn opinion*, than you prefented to the Houfe a complete ftatement of the réfources of the Bengal Government, in which you took credit for two hundred thoufand pounds a year additional refource, obtained by the expulfion of Cheyt Sing, and which it was downright *robbery* to continue to receive upon the principle of the Impeachment. As a proof that *you* entertained no idea of *his reftoration*, you gave the Houfe reafon to believe this would be a *permanent* revenue; it has *never* failed us, and is applied to the fervice of the Bombay army at this moment.

The public have received about two millions fterling *more* from Benares fince Cheyt Sing's expulfion, than they would have re-

ceived,

ceived, if he had not been expelled. Should you fay in reply, *non rapui, fed recepi*, I should imagine that thofe who think the act of expulfion originally wrong, will adopt Dean Swift's comment upon that fentence.

If I find it *impoffible* to reconcile your conduct on the fubject of Benares and the Mogul, to any idea of confiftency, I am equally at a lofs to account for what you have done as to Oude.

The arrangement which Mr. Haftings formed with the Vizier, had your *pofitive* and *repeated* approbation. Upon an idea that Sir John Macpherfon intended fome change, you wrote *moft peremptorily*, that " the agreement " formed by Mr. Haftings fhould be invaria- " bly adhered to." Could any man living believe, unlefs the fact was proved beyond

all

all doubt, that in lefs than two years from the date of fuch an approbation, you could have agreed with Mr. Burke, that it was a high crime and mifdemeanour in Mr. Haftings to form that arrangement ?

You have faid in parliament, and I agree with you moft cordially, " that India is the " brighteft jewel in the Britifh Crown ; that " we have governed India better than the " beft of the native Sovereigns now govern " it ; that fo far from dreading a decreafe in " our refources, we have every reafon to ex- " pect an increafe ; and that, before this war " broke out, there was good ground to expect " that we fhould affift Great Britain before " we required affiftance from her."

But how a perfon, profeffing fuch fentiments, can ftir *one ftep* with Mr. Burke on

the

the subject of India, is to me *incomprehensible*. Every word that *he* has ever uttered, every line that *he* has ever written, describes misery, and wretchedness, and diftress *past* and *present*, and predicts it in future, unless *Mr. Fox's Bill should be adopted.*

ASIATICUS.

Jan. 1, 1792.

L E T-

LETTER IV.

SIR,

IN order to shew the inconsistency of your
conduct as the Minister of India, I have been
obliged to mention the name of Mr. Hastings,
and to allude to the depending Impeachment,

I am aware of the delicacy of this subject,
and of the impropriety of entering into a discussion of facts, while the merit or crimi-
nality of those facts remains to be determined
in a Court of Justice.

I will, therefore, strictly confine myself to
great *political* points, and shall proceed to
shew

ſhew, that you have departed from the *ſpirit* of your own reſolutions, and from the opinions which you delivered with the utmoſt ſolemnity, in a Parliament that is no more ; and conſequently I may with propriety allude to them.

The Impeachment of Mr. Haſtings was originally reſted upon a ground which it would have ill become an enlightened Aſſembly to rejeƈt, *Humanity*. The Member who moved it, avowed moſt unequivocally, that Mr. Haſtings had reduced fertile provinces to deſarts, and a people once opulent to the loweſt ſtate of wretchedneſs and deſpair : that it was for the miſery which he had entailed upon millions that he impeached him ; but if he had *improved the reſources of the State, encouraged commerce, aided agricul-*

I   *ture,*

ture, and had *increaſed the population of the provinces committed to his government,* he never ſhould have inquired into his particular conduct, but ſhould have hailed him on his return to England as a benefactor to mankind.

I confeſs I have never reflected upon this very ſenſible part of Mr. Burke's ſpeech without aſtoniſhment, mixed with indignation, at his ſubſequent conduct.

But, as the Miniſter of India, you knew in 1786, that Mr. Haſtings *had done* all that Mr. Burke accuſed him of not having done, juſt as well as you did *in the following year,* when you unequivocally affirmed in Parliament, that the ſtate of *England,* compared to that of *India,* was as *darkneſs* oppoſed to *light;* that *Bengal* had *improved,* and was

im-

improving, under our Adminiftration. A majority of the late Parliament voted with Mr. Burke from a conviction, beyond all doubt, that the Britifh Government in Bengal had been a curfe, and not a bleffing to the people.

Mr. Burke's firft motion applied moft pointedly *to you* : it was upon the Rohilla war, which you had condemned, (and Parliament *concurred* with you) as *iniquitous, and unjuft*. The King's Minifters, including Mr. Pitt, differed completely with you on this point ; but though you affirmed, that your fentiments *were unaltered*, that you *then* thought of the *iniquity*, and *injuftice* of the war, as you had thought of it in 1782; yet, as the Legiflature had fo often appointed Mr. Haftings Governor General of Bengal *fince that war had been concluded*, you could

not

not vote it to merit Impeachment. , An argument this of very confiderable weight : but to fhew *your inconfiftency*, you never again urged it; for it might have been ufed with *juft the fame propriety* againft nine tenths of the allegations, which *you afterwards* voted to be *criminal*, as againft the Rohilla charge.

I think I can prove incontrovertibly, that the *principles* upon which you condemned the Rohilla war, would apply with *increafed force*, to the condemnation of the prefent war in India. Of this war *you* have very highly approved, and many have fuppofed you to be in fact the author of it.

It is *univerfally* agreed, that the Rohilla war originated in a breach of faith on the part of the Rohillas. *You* faid, and fo did Parliament, that *fatisfaction* might have been

G   obtained

obtained by other means than war. I believe it.

When the Britifh army was upon the
frontier of Rohilcund, there can be no doubt
of the perfect readinefs of the Rohillas, to
make confiderable facrifices to avoid the war.

And can any man in his fenfes doubt of
Tippoo's *readinefs*, and his *eagernefs* to give
the Raja of Travancore *complete fatisfaction*,
after he knew that our army was affembled
in the plains of Tritchinopoly for the attack
of his Southern poffeffions, *which he was in
no condition to defend at the time?* but is that
to be urged as a reafon for our defifting?

In the prefent war, and in the Rohilla
war then, we are to confider whether the
policy was wife or not. I have proved the
iuftice of both.

The

The profeffed object of the Rohilla war after its commencement was to annex to the Suba-fhip of Oude a territory of confiderable extent adjoining to it, bounded as Oude is, by the Ganges to the Weft, and by the fame chain of mountains to the Eaft, producing a revenue of half a million fterling a year, and under the dominion of a tribe of Afghan Tartars, the moft warlike and enterprizing people in Indoftan, who had invaded and fubdued Rohilcund in the year 1740.

To any gentleman who infpects Major Rennell's Map of Indoftan, Oude and Rohilcund will appear to be as naturally united under one Government, as the two kingdoms which are now called Great Britain. The political advantages refulting from this acceffion of dominion to Oude are no longer *fpeculative.* From the experience of feven-

G 2   teen

teen years, I am warranted in faying, that thefe advantages have been moft important indeed.

The Sovereign of Oude has been rendered more dependent upon us fince the extent of his empire. He has from that time paid more than one-third of all the expences of the Bengal army : the acquifition of Benares, and the receipt of more than fixteen millions fterling from countries beyond the Carumnaffa, had their *origin* in that Rohilla war, which you fo ftrongly condemned ; and Oude has been fecured from invafion.

The *policy*, therefore, of the Rohilla war is perfectly juftified by the experience of feventeen years,

Let me next confider the *policy* of the prefent war.

Lord

Lord Cornwallis conceived that Tippoo's antipathy to the Englifh would never be leffened, that he would feize the firft favourable moment of attack, and *therefore*, as Tippoo had given us a *juftifiable ground for* war, it was right to take advantage of the *troubles in France*, and to crufh him, or at leaft very much to reduce his power. To effect this purpofe, his Lordfhip concluded one treaty with the Marattas, and another with the Nizam; the profeffed object of both being *conqueft, and extent of dominion, for ourfelves and our allies.*

Two campaigns have already been made, and the war ftill rages. Of fuccefs, and of complete and fpeedy fuccefs, I do not doubt: but the expence has been enormoufly great: the Carnatic has been drained: Bengal has afforded above three millions fince the war com-

commenced; and more than a million in fpecie, of public and private property, has been remitted from England; and there may be very good grounds, after all, for doubting as to the *Cui Bono* of the war.

But the Rohilla war was completely finifhed in one campaign, by one brigade of the Britifh troops, and without one rupee of expence to the Company.

It would be a bad argument to ufe in defence of an unjuft war, that we gained money by it; but the Rohilla war, and the prefent war, both ftand on the fame ground of juftice, a breach of faith committed againft our allies.

It was objected to the Rohilla war, that we expelled certain Muffulman Chiefs who

lenity

had governed the natives of Rohilcund with lenity and juftice. If the origin of the war *was juft*, this objection is of no force ; *if unjuft*, it is a great and grievous aggravation *of the original crime.* The fame objection would apply againft the prefent war, if it fhould end, as it is likely to do, in the deftruction of Tippoo ; for although his avowed antipathy to all Europeans induces us to wifh the annihilation of his power, yet I do not believe that fuch an event would be of advantage to his fubjects. Savage, tyrannical, and faithlefs as he has been to us, the beft informed officers employed in the prefent fervice reprefent his country to be in the higheft ftate of cultivation, his villages very numerous, his peafantry well cloathed, well fed, attached to his Government, and happy and contented under it.

You

You are too well verſed *now* in the politics
of India, not to be aware, that no *poſſible
cloſe* of the preſent war can bring with it the
immenſe *political advantages* which reſulted
from *the Rohilla war.* I earneſtly pray, that
the *ſpeculators* of this day may, at the cloſe of
ſeventeen years, be proved to have been as much
miſtaken as the *ſpeculators* were in 1774.

The Rohilla war was pronounced by Mr.
Francis, and by the Company too, to be
founded *on wrong policy,* becauſe it increaſed
the *power* of Sujah Dowlah, and carried our
arms into countries hardly included in the
maps of Indoſtan. How futile and abſurd
muſt thoſe objections appear now to be, ſince
the fact is, that with the moſt perfect ſecu-
rity we have advanced our frontier line of
defence ſix hundred miles beyond the Carum-
naſſa; we have obtained a perpetual provi-
ſion for the pay of more than a third of

our

our army by the confequences of this annex-
ation, we have obtained wealth for the
public, and we have fecured the empire of
our ally from external attacks from 1774,
to this day.

The arguments ufed by Mr. Francis in
1774, and by the Company the next year,
were very plaufible, though, as it has turned out,
ill-founded: much more plaufible objections
have been applied againft your prefent war:
" the Marattas and Tippoo were a juft balance
" to each other, if we deftroy the one, the
" other will never be at peace with us. The
" Maratta cavalry is more numerous than
" Tippoo's. If they poffefs, upon the peace,
" the Table Land of Myfore, they will be
" ready at all times to pour down upon the
" Carnatic as Hyder was, and no force of in-
" fantry can fecure the Carnatic from the in-

H   " curfions

" incurfions of horfe." Thefe, and very
many other powerful arguments have been
urged againft this war; I hope and believe
that experience will prove them to be as ill-
founded as thofe were which you have urged,
and unhappily for this country, *with fo much
effect*, againft Mr. Haftings.

ASIATICUS.

Jan. 6, 1792.

LETTER V.

SIR,

IN the year 1785, Mr. Burke publicly' accufed you of a defign to involve our Indian
Government in impenetrable obfcurity, and
to exclude the tranfactions of the Britifh
Adminiftration in Afia, from the liberal cu-
riofity of an Englifh gentleman.*

This was a very ill-founded charge, at the
time he made it ; and in the year 1787, you
determined to lay annually before Parliament an accurate ftatement of the refources,
and political connections of Great Britain in
India.

* Mr. Burke's fpeech, February, 1785.

This

This determination was very honourable to you, although it has expofed your *incon-fiftency* in the moft glaring colours, and has afforded an additional proof of the futility of *political fpeculations*, relative *to fo diftant a dominion.*

On the 7th of May, 1787, you opened your firft budget.—It contained the following very *comfortable, and material information*:

" That Bengal was, undoubtedly, the *moft*
" *flourifhing country in India* : that it yielded a
" nett furplus revenue of *one hundred and*
" *eighty lacks*, which you were confident,
" (and here you were *correct*) would be
" increafed in the next year, *tò more than two*
" *millions fterling* : that peace was our object ;
" but that we were able to repel any *attack*,
" with a well-difciplined army of *feventy or*
" *eighty*

" *eighty thousand men*, and a surplus revenue
" of two millions, *for peace or war, if ne-*
" *cessary* : that Mr. Burke, on a former
" day, had said, " a ten years peace in India
" was too long a period to reckon on ;" but
" you could not allow, *that we were like-*
" *ly to be attacked* : there was nothing to
" tempt an enemy to attack us : there was
" no prospect of success for any power in
" India : upon what *ground* could any In-
" dian power attack us ? They would have
" to engage seventy or eighty thousand
" men, with two millions surplus revenue,
" and in case of need, another two millions
" to add to it. *The total increase of expence in*
" *the last war, amounted to no more in one year,*
" *upon an average, than two crores and three*
" *lacks, and there was no reason to suppose that*
" *any future war could be more expensive* ; for
" then we had *all India, America, and Europe,*

" *to*

" *to fight againſt : the ſurplus revenue would*
" *be ſufficient for any future war :* that you
" were as anxious as any man, not to pro-
" voke hoſtilities ; but if we *were provoked,*
" you felt a pride to ſay, that we were fully
" able to repel any attack, let it come from
" what quarter it might : that our poſſeſ-
" ſions in India, properly conſidered, *were*
" *the brighteſt jewel in the Britiſh crown."*

It is ſingular of this ſpeech, that where
you have repeated *facts,* you are moſt accurately correct.

You were equally correct in predicting the
future increaſe of our Bengal reſources,
which Mr. Haſtings had alſo foretold ſome
time before. But in ſpeculating upon the
continuance of peace, or upon the diminiſhed
expence

expence of a war, when war fhould break out, you erred moft egregioufly.

The people' of England are renowned throughout the world for fair and open dealing; for benevolence, for charity, and for an abhorrence of deceit : but Britifh politicians have often defpifed thofe ties which bind man to man in fociety; and whoever *ferioufly* reflects upon the fingular event which happened *two days -only* after you opened your India budget, muft agree with me in opinion, that *juftice, fincerity,* and *good faith,* are qualities to which fome of his Majefty's cabinet minifters cannot poffibly lay claim.

On the 7th of May, you truly affirmed that Bengal *was the moft flourifhing country in India.*

You

You took credit for an annual revenue of nearly five millions sterling, *for the fix preceding years*, and you stated very good grounds to induce Parliament to believe, that the Bengal resources would be increased in future years, as they actually were. It had happened to you *also*, to lay before Parliament, as chairman of an India committee, the actual state of the Bengal resources, for the fifteen *preceding years* ; by which, to any man who will read, the progressive increase of resources during the administration of Mr. Hastings is clearly explained. But on the 9th of May, after *a paufe of forty-eight hours*, you *concurred* with Mr. Burke in affirming in behalf of all the people of Great-Britain, that *Bengal had been defolated* ; the natives *oppreffed, and deftroyed* ; and the revenues *diminifhed* ; and that all the *extraordinary refources*, of which you had *boafted* on the 7th, were procured

cured

cured by *fraud, injuſtice, oppreſſion,* and *breach of faith.*

You well know that *I* uſe no orator's privilege; *I* neither *invent,* nor *exaggerate,* nor *miſrepreſent*; and you know it *to* be a faƈt, that of the various component parts of the Bengal reſources, *all,* except the land revenues and cuſtoms, were *created* by Mr. Haſtings, and thoſe two branches of reſources, *he improved.*

Alas ! Sir, the 7th of May could not *poſſibly* have been a *proud day for England,* as you affirmed it to be, and the 9th an unfortunate one for Mr. Haſtings, if the Miniſter of India had been aƈtuated by a ſenſe of *conſiſtency,* or *juſtice.*

In the three following years, 1788, 89, and 90, the ſame flattering accounts of the

I   *flouriſhing*

flourishing state of Bengal were repeated *by you* to the House of Commons, as regularly, as the House of Commons declared through their managers, to the *Lords* and to the *world*, that Bengal had been *ruined* by Mr. Hastings.

In each year you repeated your *confident expectation* of the *continuance of peace*; and you affirmed, and I agreed with you, " that we " had a force in India sufficient to combat all " that the whole world could bring against us, " and a surplus of revenue greater than at " any former period: that in the event of " war there were funds in India to main- " tain it, as there would have been in the " last war, if the surplus had not been em- " ployed in the purchase of investments."

How

How vain is man, when he fpeculates on politics ! !—Tippoo, on very bad terms with the Marattas and the Nizam ; abandoned by the French ; fully aware of the extent of our military force; and knowing that Lord Cornwallis had all that fupport from home, which was withheld from Mr. Haftings in the laft war; yet placed fo thorough a confidence in our moderation and love of peace, that he ventured firft to infult, and afterwards to attack the Rajah of Travancote, an ally of the Carnatic.

This attack completely juftified us in an inftant commencement of hoftilities. When Tippoo faw that we were in earneft, he changed his language; he earneftly defired us to receive a man of rank and dignity in our camp, to fettle all differences.

The

The offer was rejected, wisely rejected, in my humble opinion ; for there never was a period when, according to *human probabilities*, we had so fair an opportunity of making Tippoo smart *severely* and *quickly* for his recent conduct, and for his breach of all the important articles of Lord Macartney's Treaty.

Lord Cornwallis, in a letter to General Meadows, has stated, in the clearest language, his motives for preferring war to negociation, after Tippoo's wanton attack of the Travancore lines.

" *Good policy* (said his Lordship) as well " as a regard to *our reputation*, in this coun- " try, requires, that we should not only " *exact a severe reparation from Tippoo*, but " that we should take this *opportunity to reduce*

" *the*

" *the power of a Prince*, who avows, *upon*
" *every occasion*, so rancorous an enmity *to*
" *our nation.*

" At present we have every prospect of
" *aid* from the *Country Powers*, whilst *he can*
" *expect no assistance from France*, &c. &c."

It appears then, that you were mistaken in
supposing that no Country Power *would*
presume to provoke us, and being provoked,
we have preferred rightly, so I think, war
to peace.

The next point in which you have erred
is, as to the expence of the war ; according
to your *declared opinion*, no future war could
be more expensive than the last. But beyond all doubt the present war exceeds that
of the last, in expence, to a degree, that

cannot

cannot be calculated at prefent, becaufe.
there is no account, that I know of, of the
quantity of Bills that have been drawn
upon Bengal in the year 1791, nor will
many of the contingent expences of the war
be liquidated until after the reftoration of
peace. Some perfons with whom I have
converfed, have carried their ideas of the
expences of the war far beyond any that I
entertain ; but I can fpeak to fome points
from tolerable information. From the month
of April, 1790, to the month of January,
1791, a period of nine months, Bengal fup-
plied Fort St. George and Bombay with more
than two hundred and twenty lacks of rupees in money, accepted bills, provifions and
ftores ; five hundred thoufand pounds were
remitted to Madras laft year, of public money,
and as much more, the property of individuals ; fixty or feventy thoufand pounds

were

were taken from the China ships of 1790;
and money was borrowed at Madras, nearly,
I believe, to the amount of one hundred
thousand pounds. Bills also have been
drawn from India, but to what amount I
cannot say. General Meadows began his
operations in the month of June, 1790.
We have no later intelligence from the
Grand Army than the 8th of July, 1791,
little more than thirteen months from the
commencement of the war. Lord Cornwallis, as we learn from the Gazette, wanted
a very large supply of provisions, stores of every
kind, twenty-six thousand bullocks, with
half that number of drivers, or his bullocks,
he said, would be *useless*. These supplies
could not possibly be obtained from a country so exhausted as the Carnatic, without involving individuals in considerable distress,
and

and without a material deduction from the public revenue.

I do not pretend to guefs at the amount of the firft year's expence, and of fo many months of the fecond year, as may be required to bring the war to a fuccefsful termination ; but every Gentleman who confiders the materials of which we are all in poffeffion, muft agree with me, that it would be an act of the groffeft folly and abfurdity to compare the heavy expences of this war, carried on againft a *fingle* Power, with the *inconfiderable difburfements* of the laft war, when all Europe, and all India, were united for our deftruction.

ASIATICUS.

Jan. 11, 1792.

SIR,

THOUGH the annual expence of this war has very confiderably exceeded the annual charge of the laft, I do not impute the excefs to any want of œconomy in Lord Cornwallis, or any other officer who has commanded a Britifh army, fince the commencement of hoftilities.

Lord Cornwallis, both in America and in India, has been a rigid œconomift of the public money; the excefs is owing *to a total change of fyftem at home*; a change which was effected contrary to the wifhes of the Eaft India Company.

K   The

The *effective force*, and the *compoſition* of our *Indian armies*, has been totally *altered* ſince the cloſe of the laſt war : it was an idea from which no officer bred in the Company's ſervice could depart, that a regiment of European infantry, with eight battalions of Sepoys, would have defeated any force that could be collected to oppoſe them by a native power. Sir Eyre Coote had not ſeven thouſand infantry, and leſs than two thouſand of this number were Europeans, when he totally defeated Hyder Ally Cawn at Porto Novo in 1781, although the latter had acquired confidence from recent ſucceſſes ; nor did Sir Eyre command ten thouſand infantry in the field at any one period of the laſt war.

General Goddard's army was formed upon a more contracted ſcale than Sir Eyre Coote's ; the

the armies commanded by Colonel Muir, Colonel Camac, and Colonel Popham, in the late war, would now be called inconfiderable detachments, and they were compofed entirely of native troops, with the exception of a few European artillerymen to work their guns,

I had infinite pleafure in hearing the panegyric which you once pronounced upon the late Lord Clive, from whom I confefs that I have picked up moft of my military ideas of India fervice ; what would that enlightened ftatefman and foldier have conceived of your favourite fyftem, of defending *Bengal*, by keeping up enormous military eftablifhments at *Fort St. George* and *Bombay ?* In the year 1766, when the Marattas were *united* under a powerful Prince, and in fact the only native power of any confequence in India, his Lord-

K 2   fhip

ſhip ſpeaks of them and of us in the following terms :

" At preſent *they* are the only power who
" can excite diſturbances in Bengal, nor have
" we any thing further than a mere temporay
" interruption to our collections to appre-
" hend, *even from the Marattas* ; ſince, with
" our *well diſciplined*, and *numerous army*, we
" may bid defiance to the moſt powerful
" *country army*, that *can be brought* into the
" field."

The *numerous army* of Lord Clive, was
three regiments of European infantry, eigh-
teen battalions of Seapoys, and three troops
of Mogul cavalry, with a field and battering
train, and five companies of European artil-
lery ; one third of this force was ſtationed in
Allahabad,

Allahabad, another third in the Bahar Province, and the remainder in Bengal.

The large armies that have been brought into the field fince this war commenced, *and the very great increafe of Europeans in the compofition of thofe armies,* has added greatly to the expence, and indeed in the nature of things muft have carried it far beyond the charges incurred in the laft war, when an eftablifhment of *fix thoufand feven hundred bullocks,* for an army of thirty thoufand men, excited the *wonder* and *cenfure* of an *enlightened Houfe of Commons!*

When you affirmed, *in two fuccelfive years,* that no future war could be fo expenfive as the laft, you affigned, as a reafon in fupport of your opinion, that we had *then, Europe, America,* and *India* againft us, *which*

I   *could*

could never happen again. But you fhould have confidered, that the expences of war do not depend upon the number of our enemies, but upon the quantum of force that we fhall oppofe to thofe enemies, and the ftate of the country in which our operations are carried on. The expence of the late predatory war in America almoft defied calculation.

The extraordinaries of the American army exceeded each year the annual amount of all our Indian military expences, during fo extended a warfare, and for this obvious reafon, becaufe the troops in America were chiefly fed from Leadenhall market ; Lord Cornwallis has drawn every article of fub-fiftence, almoft, from the Carnatic, and Bengal, fince he invaded Myfore, which, of courfe, has materially fwelled the difburfe-ments in the prefent war.

When

When you made your affertion, the chances were fifty to one in your favour that there would no be war in India in your time, or mine, and therefore you could rifque any pre-diction relative to war expences with very tolerable fecurity.

In thefe letters I have attempted with fair-nefs, candour, and moderation, to lay before the public a feries of inconfiftencies, which, for the credit of Britifh politics, cannot, I truft, be equalled in our hiftory. I fhall clofe my correfpondence with an additional in-ftance of your inconfiftency, which is, in its nature, fo very extraordinary, that I fcarcely expect any gentleman will give entire credit to it, until he has examined the various docu-ments to which I fhall refer him, with the fame attention that I have beftowed upon them.

I muft

I muſt of neceſſity again allude to the political tranſactions of Mr. Haſtings, in order to ſhew that it will be impoſſible to reconcile to common ſenſe, or to any man's idea of conſiſtency, your complete and entire approbation of the meaſures purſued ſince this war commenced, with your pointed condemnation of Mr. Haſtings in the moſt critical moment of the laſt war.

I muſt take the fact to be as you and Mr. Pitt have affirmed it, by your ſpeeches and your votes in the laſt Parliament ; that Mr. Haſtings violated the moſt ſolemn treaties when he demanded a ſubſidy from Cheyt Sing in the laſt war, and when he concluded the treaty of Chunar with the Nabob of Oude. Theſe were acts which by Mr. Pitt's aſſertion " No State Neceſſity could juſtify."

And

After admitting the violation of public treaties in both inftances, and admitting alfo that no ftate neceffity could juftify fuch atrocious proceedings, I fhall firft fhew the fort of neceffity under which Mr. Haftings laboured, when he concluded the treaty of Chunar, and then I will prove that in your adminiftration, treaties have been avowedly violated, and that the violation has received your *complete and entire approbation*,

Great Britain was engaged in war with America, France, Spain, and Holland, in the year 1781, and fome of the wifeft politicians in England expected a national bankruptcy. In India we were at war with the Marattas and Hyder Ally Cawn. The King's Minifters had informed Mr. Haftings that France intended to make the moft vigorous efforts to regain that confequence

L   which

which she had once held as a nation in India, and that Holland would of courfe affift her in carrying fo great a point, to the utmoft of her power.

Sir Eyre Coote, who commanded the Britifh army in the Carnatic, wrote to Mr. Haftings, that he depended upon him for feven lacks of rupees a month, and provifions and ftores, for the fupply of the forces which were then oppofed to Hyder Ally Cawn.

General Goddard and Colonel Muir, who commanded the armies oppofed to the Pefh-wa's troops, and to Madajee Scindia, depended alfo upon Bengal for fupport. The Company had pofitively interdicted Mr. Haftings from drawing bills upon England; and as a confiderable debt had been

incurred

incurred upon bond, and the bonds were at a great difcount, further loans upon bonds were *impracticable*. Under fuch circumftances Mr. Haftings left Calcutta in July 1781, and a celebrated orator has reprefented him on this occafion, in the character of a highwayman, hefitating whether he fhould take the road to Finchley, or Hounflow, a fpecies of rhetoric *perfectly new, indictum ore alio,* and equally applicable to the moft virtuous, as to the moft flagitious actions. Two modes of fupply were open to him ; the firft, a fine to be levied upon the Zemindar of Benares ; the fecond, the immediate receipt of a very large fum of money due from the Nabob of Oude to the Eaft India Company.

From Benares no money was procured, though by the expulfion of Cheyt Sing, the Company gained two hundred thoufand

pounds

pounds a year, and several reftrictions were laid upon the new Zemindar. His rights were accurately defined, and his dependance upon Bengal unequivocally acknowledged.

From the Nabob of Oude, Mr. Haftings procured, three months after the treaty of Chunar was figned, the fum of fifty-five lacks, and within the year the fum of one hundred and thirty-eight lacks of rupees.

He muft be a child in India knowledge who is not convinced that the Britifh empire was faved by thefe extraordinary fupplies. You once unequivocally allowed the fact to be fo; and the Eaft India Company, with the *concurrence of Mr. Pitt*, acknowledged that the exertions of Mr. Haftings preferved India; but the very great

impor-

importance of the fervice performed, when a large fupply of ready money was procured, and the immenfe permanent advantages obtained for the nation, by the expulfion of Cheyt Sing, and by the treaty of Chunar, could not change the nature of the two tranfactions. In both cafes, Mr. Haftings " *grofsly violated the public faith, difgraced and* " *degraded the Britifh nation, and gave up its* " *honour.*" So thinking, you felt yourfelf at perfect liberty, *honourably* and *confcientioufly* to condemn Mr. Haftings on *one day* for thefe outrageous acts, and on *another* to congratulate the nation on the importance and value of refources, which, though thus *fraudulently* and *difgracefully* obtained, had made our fituation fo flourifhing in India, that it was, when compared with the ftate of Great Britain, as *light* oppofed to *darknefs*.

From

From Minifters whofe confciences are fo tender, who have been fo jealous of *the national honour*; and who laid it down as *their firft principle*, that *treaties* concluded in India fhould be *inviolably obferved*; the world will naturally expect the moft *rigid adherence* to engagements which they have themfelves ordered to be entered into, and which they have very warmly approved of.

I will ftate, therefore, the *letter and fpirit* of the treaties concluded *under your orders* with the Nabob of Arcot, and the Rajah of Tanjore: I will fhew the *manner* in which they have been *violated*, and then I will leave it to the world to determine, whether, confiftently with the principles you have invariably profeffed as the Minifter of India, you could, *under any cirumftances*, have given your *complete and entire approbation* to the infraction of *thofe treaties*.   .   ASIATICUS.

Jan. 16, 1792.

LETTER VII.

SIR,

THE feizure of the government of the Car-natic, and of Tanjore, in violation of two fo-lemn treaties, could not poffibly have re-ceived your *complete and entire approbation*, without an utter abandonment of every *prin-ciple* that you have ever profeffed upon India tranfactions.

Of the propriety of the meafure, either as it refpects Lord Cornwallis or General Mea-dows, I do not prefume even to inquire; *they* have neither moved *refolutions* in Parlia-ment, nor pledged themfelves to obferve in-

violably

violably *any particular line of conduct*, you have done both,

It has been ufual upon all proper occaſions, for his Majefty's Minifters to fpeak of the public fervices of Sir A. Campbell, the late Governor of Fort St. George, in the ftrongeft poffible terms. When Lord Grenville was in the Houfe of Commons, he affirmed, that the nation owed obligations to Sir A. Campbell, which it could never repay, and in the Houfe of Peers, the fame Noble Lord mentioned his name with every mark of refpect in the laft year, and lamented his death, as a very great national misfortune.

Having had the honour to know Sir A. Campbell, many years ago, when he was chief engineer in Bengal, I cannot but be

pleafed

pleafed that his feryices were fo warmly and publicly acknowledged.

Not meaning to infinuate that any part of Sir A. Campbell's conduct, as Governor of Fort St. George, was void of merit, it will be fully admitted, that the only important meafures of his adminiftration were, 1ft, His fpirited conduct, when Tippoo, in the years 1787 and 1788, menaced the Rajah of Travancore with an invafion : and 2d, His treaties with the Nabob of Arcot, and the Rajah of Tanjore.

It is to the fubject of thefe treaties that I fhall confine my remarks, and if Sir A. Campbell had infinite merit in concluding them, I do not fee how you can be free from blame, in having completely and intirely approved the infraction of them.

M   In

In the course of the last war, the Nabob of the Carnatic surrendered his revenues, and his country to Lord Macartney; he soon repented of this act, and tried in vain to get his dominions back again, until *you* became the Minister of India, and restored them,

b. The Rajah of Tanjore retained his country throughout the war, although Mr. Haftings had urged Lord Macartney to apply all the public refources of Tanjore, to the public fervice, as long as the war fhould continue.

c. Such a fentiment from Mr. Haftings ftruck you with fo much *horror*, that in the fpring of 1782, in the Rockingham Administration, you moved the following Refolutions, which

2   were

were voted *unanimously* by the House of Commons:

29th April. " That any attempts to seize " upon the revenues of the kingdom of Tan- " jore, and to confiscate the same for the pur- " pose of the Nabob, *or of the* East India " Company, is contrary to the public faith, " and tends to the *oppression* and *ruin* of the " country."

28th May. " That *if any person, in viola-* " *tion of the public faith*, given *by the East* " *India Company in* 1775, and contrary to " the *true intent* and *meaning* of the several " Resolutions of this House, of the 29th of " April last, have taken, *in sequestration or* " *otherwise*, the revenues of Tanjore, into " the management of the Nabob of Arcot, " *or of the East India Company*, it is the duty

M 2   " of

" of the Court of Directors, *forthwith*, to
" order the said revenues to be returned to
" the administration of the King of Tanjore,
" *agreeable to the treaties of the years* 1762
" *and* 1775."

In conformity to the spirit of these resolutions; after you became the Minister of India,
you ordered Sir A. Campbell, to conclude
one Treaty with the Nabob of Arcot, and
another with the Rajah of Tanjore ; the orders were obeyed, and the treaties were concluded in February 1787.

The various articles in these treaties are
worded with so much clearness and perspi-
cuity, that it is impossible for a man who can
read to mistake their letter or their spirit.

The

The meaning is most evidently this, that under no possible circumstances should the Company seize upon the revenues and government of the Carnatic and Tanjore : but if by mismanagement on the part of the Nabob, or the Rajah, they should fail in their stipulated payments, then certain measures were to be taken in order to secure the Company ; the extent of these measures was most accurately defined, and beyond that extent *the Company could not go*, without a direct breach of the treaties.

The preamble to each Treaty states in substance, " That peace being happily re-esta-" blished in the Carnatic, the present hour " is considered as best suited for settling " and arranging, by a *just* and *equitable* trea-" ty, a plan for the future defence and pro-" tection of the Carnatic." After this sensi-

ble

ble exordium, it is stated, " that the Nabob
" and the Rajah shall pay a specific sum an-
" nually, for the military peace establish-
" ment of the Carnatic."

It is farther stated, " that in war, four-
" fifths of their revenue shall be appropriated
" for the service of the war."—It is also
agreed, " that in peace, whenever the pay-
" ments fall one month in arrear, the Com-
" pany shall have a claim upon the revenues
" of certain specified districts, and shall have
" power to send superintendants into those
" specified districts, who shall receive the
" rents from the *Nabob's Aumils*. That if
" the Aumils behave ill, the Nabob shall
" dismiss them, and appoint such others as
" the Governor and Council shall recom-
" mend." It is farther specified, that when
" the

" the arrears are paid up, the Company's fu-
" perintendants fhall be recalled."

In the event of war, " the Company are
" to fend infpectors to fee that four-fifths of
" the revenues are honeftly applied to the pub-
" lic fervice, and the Nabob has the *fame*
" *privilege* of appointing infpectors, in order
" to be convinced that four-fifths of *the Com-*
" *pany's revenues* are applied with the fame
" fidelity to the public fervice." It is farther
agreed, " that if the Nabob diverts any part
" of the four-fifths of his revenues from the
" public fervice, then the Company may
" fend *fuperintendants*, who are to receive
" the revenues *from his Aumils*." After all
thefe provifions are made with as much per-
fpicuity as our language, or any language
can admit of, it is *expreffly* faid, " that the
" exercife of *power* over the faid diftricts and
" farms,

" farms, in cafe of *failure*, fhall not *extend*,
" or be *conftrued to extend, to deprive his*
" Highnefs the Nabob of the Carnatic, in be-
" half of himfelf or his fucceffors, of the Civil
" Government thereof, the credit of his family,
" or the dignity of his illuftrious Houfe, but
" that *the fame fhall be preferved to him and*
" *them inviolable, faving and excepting* the
" *powers* in the foregoing article *expreffed* and
" mentioned."

There is another very fair ftipulation, that
if there fhould be an effential failure in the
crops from want of rain, or any unforefeen
calamity, there fhall be a deduction in the
payment tantamount to the injury received.

Such is the treaty concluded, *under your
own orders*, with the Nabob, (and that with
the Rajah is fimilar to it) in which every thing
that

that *could happen*, either in *peace* or in *war*, is *expreſſly provided for.*

To give additional *ſolemnity* to this treaty, Sir John Macpherſon and Mr. Stables, who were at Madras, on their way to England at that time, were preſent when it was ſigned, and witneſſed its execution.

Sir A. Campbell, in a letter to the Directors, details the various ſteps that he took previous to the concluſion of this treaty, and he ſpeaks in the following warm terms of the Nabob:

" I have narrowly watched the Nabob's " *conduct* and *ſentiments* ſince my arrival in " this country, *and I am ready to declare,* " that I do not think it poſſible that any " *Prince* or *power on earth*, can be more

N " *ſincerely*

" *sincerely attached* to the prosperity of the
" Honourable Company than his Highness,
" *or that any one has a higher claim to their*
" *favour and liberality.*"

The conclusion of this treaty appeared to
be a point of such importance, and such
was your sense of Sir A. Campbell's services
in effecting your object, that, after the period
for the sailing of a packet was passed, you
promise, in a postscript to the general letter,
to reply particularly to the Fort St. George
dispatches, by the next season, and then you
add these words :

" But we cannot omit embracing the *ear-*
" *liest opportunity* of expressing *our warmest*
" *approbation* of the manner in which OUR
" ORDERS, relative to the treaty with the
" Na-

" Nabob of Arcot, *have been carried into exe-*
" *cution*."

After fo marked an approbation from the
Minifter of India, the Nabob and the Rajah
might well believe, that nothing would have
induced you to violate thefe treaties.

They well knew that you had very feverely
cenfured Mr. Haftings, upon the Journals of
Parliament, for preffing Lord Macartney to
apply the refources of Tanjore to the public
fervice during the late war, becaufe it was
contrary to " *public faith,* and tended to the
" *oppreffion* and *ruin of the country*, to feize
" the *government.*

They *knew* that your tender regard *for
Britifh honour*, had induced *you* to impeach
Mr. Haftings, for a fuppofed violation of faith,

although

although no Prince, or power in India, complained againſt him, on this, or on any other head. They *knew* that *your treaties* provided expreſsly *for every contingency* that could happen, both *in peace in war* ; and and they *knew* that *no poſſible* event could juſtify you in ſeizing their dominions ; of courſe they could not *believe*, that under *any circumſtances, you* would have *degraded*, *diſgraced*, and *diſhonoured*, both them and the Britiſh nation.

ASIATICUS,

18th Jan. 1792.

LETTER VIII.

SIR,

AT the time the Nabob of Arcot signed the treaty, he informed Sir Archibald
Campbell that he had taken a very heavy
burthen of expence upon himself; and soon
after Sir A. Campbell's departure from Madras, he represented in very strong terms to
Lord Cornwallis the impoverished state of the
Carnatic, and his own difficulties in paying
so large a sum annually to the Company and
his creditors.

Thefe representations, if they were founded in truth, confirmed the sentiments that
were delivered in Parliament some years ago
by your friend Mr. Burke.

The

The Nabob paid the fums that he had ftipulated to difcharge for two years; but in March 1790, which was in the third year of the treaty, he fell fix lacks and a half of pagodas in arrears.

By the letter of the treaty, the Madras Government might have infifted upon the Nabob's affigning to them certain diftricts, the revenues of which they might have received from the Nabob's Aumils, until the arrear had been paid up; but they were in the moft pofitive terms precluded from interfering in the civil government of the country.

This ftep they did not take, and General Meadows, the month after his acceffion to the Government, wrote to the Directors in the following terms :

31ſt March, 1790, " We have a long ar-
" rear both from and to us. His Highneſs
" the Nabob is ſo backward in his payments,
" and oppreſſive to his Polegars, that at
" this time it is ſo neceſſary to have on our
" ſide, that *I conceive* it will be *abſolutely ne-*
" *ceſſary*, upon his firſt material delay of pay-
" ment, *to take the management of his country*
" *into your own hands* ; a meaſure, in ſpite of
" the oppoſition to it, ſo advantageous to you,
" the country, and even to his Highneſs him-
" ſelf, when ſo wiſely projected and ably ex-
" ecuted by Lord Macartney."

I do not mean to queſtion the propriety
of ſuch ſentiments as coming from General
Meadows, who expected, when he wrote the
letter, that he ſhould want two hundred and
forty thouſand pounds a month for the pay
of his army. But I would aſk you, where
then

then is the boasted faith of Great Britain *under your administration?* What *consistency* can *you lay* claim to? At the very moment that you are prosecuting *one Governor,* because, as *you* think, he violated a treaty *when surrounded with difficulties,* you have given your *complete* and *entire approbation* to General Meadows, who *really* and *truly,* and in *substance* says, "We have a treaty with the Nabob, "by which certain provisions are made for "our security, provided he fails in his pay- "ment. The provisions are *inadequate,* and "*therefore* it is absolutely necessary, *we should* "*break the treaty.*"

What adds to my wonder on this occasion is, that *you* who are so jealous of the honour and good faith of Great Britain in India, that you would not allow Tippoo to attack an inconsiderable Chief beyond the extreme

point

point of the Carnatic, becaufe he was our ally, yet approve *completely* and *entirely* of an avowed breach of faith with the oldeft ally of England in India, with a Prince who has been in conftant correfpondence with his late, and prefent Majefty, and who fhared with us in our earlieft ftruggles for empire, under Lawrence, Clive, and Coote; nay, you firft approved of a war originating from a *conftructive breach of treaty*, and then ratified, and thereby made your own, *a direct and avowed breach of treaty* committed in the very commencement of it.

In the letter from the Madras Government to the Court of Directors, which is before the Houfe of Commons, they detailed the various applications that they had made to the Nabob, for the balance due to them according to the ftipulations in Sir A.

O

Camp-

Campbell's treaty; and war being in fact
inevitable, and their army equipping for the
field, they *candidly*, and *fairly* say, (in their
letter to Bengal) " We proceeded to re-
" mark *on the insufficiency* of the stipulations
" *in Sir Archibald Campbell's treaty*, to secure
" the regular receipt of 4-5ths of the Nabob's
" revenues, agreed to be paid to the Com-
" pany's treasury, *in the event of war*."

They say further, " With this view we
" pointed out to his Lordship in council,
" *the impolicy of depending for our principal re-*
" *sources,* at a time *when the greatest exertions*
" *were necessary, and pecuniary supplies of the*
" *utmost importance,* upon the operation and ma-
" *nagement of the* Nabob's Government, of
" which the system was perhaps as defective
" and insufficient as any upon earth ; and
" we did not hesitate to declare it, *as our*
" *unqua-*

" *unqualified opinion*, that this Government
" *ought*, during the war, *to take the Nabob's*
" *country under their own management*, as af-
" fording the only means by which the re-
" fources to be derived from it could be
" realized, and the fidelity and attachment
" of the Polegars, and tributaries fecured,
" which is of the utmoft importance to the
" fuccefsful operations of the war.

" In the event of his Lordfhip's agreeing
" with us in opinion, and inftructing us to
" act in conformity, we fubmitted to him
" the *neceffity* of our adopting the meafure,
" *in fo comprehenfive a manner, as to preclude*
" *any kind of interference on the part of the Na-*
" *bob, while* the country was under our ma-
" nagement, and ftating that if this *were not*
" *done, the expected advantages would not be*
" *derived.*"

All

All that can be said of this reasoning is, that, according to the opinion of the Madras Government, Sir Archibald Campbell had concluded an inefficient, foolish treaty, and that there was an absolute NECESSITY *to violate it.* As to the Nabob's not ruling his country *well*, it must be allowed, at least, that he governed it upon the same principles in 1790, *when we broke the treaty*, as in 1787, *when we made the treaty*; and if we are to make *a pensioner* of every Sovereign in India, who does not govern his dominions so well as we have ruled Bengal, I will take upon me to say, that there will not be one independent Prince throughout Indostan and Deccan.

In fact, the present Government of Madras has pronounced Sir Archibald Campbell's treaty to be *radically defective.* I hope

I   Lord

Lord Grenville will be his defender, since his Lordship has publicly declared, " that " this country owed obligations to Sir Ar- " chibald Campbell, which she never can " repay."

I hope *you* also will justify *your own orders*, for the treaty is *your's*, and not Sir Archi- bald's, since the moment you heard that it was concluded, you, in the name of the Court of Directors, wrote to him, " that " you could not omit embracing the earliest " opportunity of expressing your *warmest* " *approbation* of the manner in which *your* " *orders*, relative to the treaty with the Na- " bob of Arcot, had been carried into exe- " cution."

The Government of Bengal say, in reply to the representation from Madras, " that " the

" the resources of Bengal, exhausted as
" they are by drains of various kinds, du-
" ring a long series of successive years,
" could not long support such expences as
" those with which the present war must be
" attended," even were the Nabob punctual
in his payments ; and they add, that unless
the whole, or great part of the heavy arrears are paid off, and the proportion of the
Nabob and the Rajah punctually discharged
in future, " we not only foresee great im-
" mediate embarrassment to the Company's
" finances, but also much ground for ap-
" prehension, that the ultimate success of the
" war may be greatly endangered."

They proceed therefore to authorize the
Madras Board to assume the *revenues* and *go-*
vermment, both of the Carnatic and Tanjore.

You

You will observe, that throughout this transaction, neither the Madras, nor the Bengal Government, pretend that they are acting agreeably either to the *letter* or the *spirit* of Sir Archibald Campbell's treaties.

But to put this matter out of all doubt, I shall transcribe the following passages of a letter from General Medows and his Council to Bengal, which will shew the opinion *they* entertained of these treaties:

12th May, 1790, " It might have been *ex-* " *pected*, that the securities for the perform- " ance of the war stipulations, which are of " such importance, would have been made " *stronger* than those which are provided in " the event of failures in the time of peace, " but they are, in fact, *less efficient*, and the " process

"'procefs prefcribed for failures in time of
war, is fo tedious and complicated, *that it*
" *can fcarce be faid to deferve the name of any*
" *fecurity or provifion whatever.*"

" If the profecution of a vigorous war,
" and the defence of the country, *are to de-*
" *pend upon us,* we conceive it *felf-evident,*
" that we *mufl have recourfe to modes very dif-*
" *ferent from thofe prefcribed by Sir A. Camp-*
" *bell's treaty.*"

The Madras Government firft endeavoured
to *perfuade* the Nabob to refign his government during the war, and until the arrears
were paid off. This, at it was very natural to
believe, was a vain attempt. He profeffed
the utmoft aftonifhment at the attempt, but
offered to receive infpectors, agreeably to
the *letter* and fpirit of Sir Archibald Campbell's

bell's treaty. To this the acting Governor replied, " that the powers *vested by the treaty,* " in the appointment of inspectors, *were not* " *judged adequate.*"

The Nabob again offered to receive in-spectors, *agreeable to the treaty*, and added, " I cannot allow myself for one moment to " suppose, that while our whole force is " directed against our inveterate enemy, " *whose fall aggrandizes two new allies of the* " *Company*, the Supreme Government should " mean to dispossess the old and faithful ally " of the King of Great Britain, the English " nation, and the Company, *of his domi-* " *nions.*"

These remonstrances he repeats very often, and calls upon the Madras Government to

P abide

abide by the treaty. "His Highnefs" (they fay in a letter to Bengal) " will confent to the " Company's Collectors being fent, *agreeably* " *to the treaty*, which, *he knows*, is confi- " dered *by us*, as *infufficient fecurity.*"

' The Nabob holds out to the laft, and in his clofing letter he fays, "In the mean " time, I repeat, and now probably for " the laft time on this occafion, that I fhall " continue to exercife the government of " my country, and enforce obedience to my " orders, as the legal, and acknowledged " Sovereign. I inclofe you a copy of the " orders I have iffued to my Aumildars in " confequence of the meafures you have " taken."

Thefe

These orders were a recital of the material articles of his late treaty with the English. He then says, that he has offered to fulfil the condition of the treaty, but that the Madras Government are determined to break it; and he orders his Aumlidars to obey no directions, but from himself.

Immediately after this circular letter was sent, the Nabob was deprived of his country, so was the Rajah of Tanjore, and both have *strongly*, but *ineffectually* appealed for redress to those Ministers, who are now prosecuting Mr. Hastings *for breach of faith* to an *ally of Great Britain.*

I will *prove*, in my next letter, that in giving entire and *complete approbation* to these

P 2   mea-

meafures, you have abandoned *all your principles,* and all your *profeffions,* as a Minifter
of India.

ASIATICUS,

21 *Jan.* 1792.

LET-

LETTER IX.

SIR,

WERE Mr. Pitt to propose a tax bill in the House of Commons, to argue long and ably in defence of it, and then to divide with those who opposed it ; with all our respect for the privilege of Parliament, we could hardly avoid taking notice of such monstrous inconsistency.

You have proposed *resolutions*, and Parliament has voted them ; *you* have laid down *certain principles*, as the *fixed* and *unalterable principles*, by which India ought to be governed, and you have *abandoned* those principles completely.

Not

Not all the *public services* of Mr. Haftings could fcreen him from your cenfure in the two laft Parliaments, " becaufe he had vio-
" lated the *public* faith, and feemed more am-
" bitious of the character of an *Alexander* or
" an *Aurungzebe*, than of the peaceable re-
" prefentative *of a company of merchants.*"

I admit moft fully, that thinking as you profeffed to do of Mr. Haftings, your affent to his impeachment was ftrictly conformable to the *principles*, which are contained in your refolutions, but recent events have convinced the world, that the *code of laws* which you framed for the guidance of *others*, have been utterly *difregarded* by yourfelf.

I have proved, beyond the poffibility of a cavil or difpute, that the only two treaties, concluded by *your own orders*, and ftamped

by

by your *warmeft approbation*, have been avowedly violated, and that you have *completely
and entirely approved* of the violation of both.

When the fubject was mentioned in the
laft Seffion, and when a Member pledged
himfelf to prove the facts, you boldly declared, that every ftep taken by Lord Cornwallis and General Medows was *warranted
by treaties*, and that the Member who had
pledged himfelf to prove the reverfe, had offered a pledge, *which he never could redeem*.
In that manly, decifive ftyle, which dif-
tinguifhes your fpeeches, you declared that
you fhould be totally barred *from every plea
of defence*, if it fhould be proved to the public, that you had *any fhare* in approving a
breach of treaty *by others*, while you voted
for the *continuance* of the Impeachment of
Mr. Haftings, *on that particular point*.

What

What *man* could fay more? fuch fentiments would do credit to a man of honour.
But what *a miferable clofe* has followed *fo fpirited an opening!!*

The papers which prove the violation of
treaties, by the candid *acknowledgement* of
thofe who *did violate them*, are before the public, and both Houfes of Parliament; the facts
were fully and ably ftated, both by Lord
Portchefter, the Marquis of Lanfdown, and
Lord Stormont, and the truth of the facts
was fully admitted by the Lord Chancellor,
as indeed they muft be by every man, who
will not prefer the *affertion* of the Minifter of
India to the evidence of his own fenfes.

Lord Grenville, who defended the juftice
of the war in India, with great ability and
with powerful eloquence, wifely ch of

caft

caſt a veil over the breach of the two treaties,
though " he lamented the death of Sir Ar-
" chibald Campbell, one of the *ableſt, honeſt-*
" *eſt, and moſt upright ſervants of the Com-*
" *pany,* who had ended a moſt honourable
" life, and was no longer in a ſituation of
" enjoying what would have been to him,
" above all things, gratifying, viz. *the appro-*
" *bation of both Houſes of Parliament.*"

Miniſters are certainly framed of very
different materials from *common mortals* ; were
I to adopt as my own opinion of the Nabob
of Arcot, that profeſſed by Sir A. Campbell,
and were I next to take *General Medows's*
character of *the ſame Prince* ; were *I* to ſay
that *one Governor* deſerved *my warmeſt appro-*
bation for concluding a *treaty* with him, *on a*
ſolid and laſting foundation, and that *another*
Governor deſerved my approbation *alſo for*

Q   *breaking*

breaking it, becaufe it was fo *loofe,* and *ineffi-cient* as to be *ufelefs;* I fhould either be laugh-ed at as an idiot, or defpifed as a knave.

To complete this fubject, I muft ftate *the circumflances of the times,* when Mr. Haftings, according *to your ideas,* violated certain trea-ties, for which he is *now under profecution,* with your concurrence, and when the prefent Governments in India violated treaties, for which you have tranfmitted to them, in con-junction with Mr. Pitt, *your complete and en-tire approbation.* '

In the year 1781, we were, as you well know, at war with all the great powers of In-dia and Europe; Mr. Haftings's *motive* for concluding the treaty of Chunar has not even been doubted. It was to obtain the *earlieft poffible payment* of a very large fum of

2   money,

money, and he fucceeded; but to urge the
Nabob of Oude to refume the treafures in his
mother's poffeffions, and to feize her Jag-
hires, was to forfeit the guarantee of the
Company, confequently *to violate a folemn
Treaty*, and of courfe to *difgrace* and to *de-
grade* the *honour of Great Britain*.

The only *poffible motive* that could have
induced Mr. Haftings to advife Lord Macartney, in the fame year, 1781, to apply the
revenues of Tanjore to the public fervice,
was to procure every rupee that could be
fcraped together, in that moft trying hour of
difficulty and danger.

For the advice, *you* cenfured him by a
Parliamentary refolution; for procuring a
large fum of money from Oude, *you impeached him*, becaufe he *violated a folemn treaty*.

Will

Will you venture, Sir, to tell the public, that India was in the same critical state in 1790, *when your treaties were violated*, as it was in 1781, when the treaty of Chunar was signed? I will take upon me to affirm, that you will not.

In 1781, with exhausted resources, we had a war to maintain in every quarter of India; and peace was only to be procured by the most vigorous and spirited exertions; for, without wasting your time or mine, by a discussion of the wisdom *of your resolutions*, I can assure you that *in India*, it is not the mode of getting a peace, to tell the whole world, as you did, *that we were unable to carry on the war, and that we were the aggressors originally.*

The

The diftrefs *at home* in 1781 was very ferious alfo; the nation, or rather the Minifters and Parliament, ftill perfifted in the fatal American conteft, and all Europe rejoiced at our folly. Mr. Haftings could not venture to draw bills upon England, and if he had, there were, as he well knew, no affets in Leadenhall Street to difcharge them. Reduced at laft to the neceffity either of putting a total ftop to the inveftment, or drawing bills to the amount of it, he adopted the latter expedient, and though the goods he fent to England *fold for a confiderable profit*, yet in the *Portland adminiftration*, when the confcientious Sir Henry Fletcher was the chairman, and when his Grace, and Lord John Cavendifh had, *by law,* the *infpection* and *approval* of all letters, the Directors wrote a very fevere cenfure to Mr. Haftings for drawing thofe bills, and told him, that " he

" *muft*

" *muſt fall upon ſome other mode of ſupplying*
" *the public exigencies.*"

In 1790 the caſe was totally changed.
We had had a ſix years peace. The reſources
of Bengal, Benares, and Oude, had improved
far beyond *your* moſt ſanguine expectation,
and even the predictions that *I* had ventured
to make, *were more than fulfilled.* The ſuc-
ceſsful ſtruggle that we had made in the
late war againſt a hoſt of foes, had very con-
ſiderably added to the reputation of Great
Britain in India. In Bengal and in Oude ſhe
was unaſſailable, and her receipts exceeded
her expences above two millions ſterling a
year.

At Madras and Bombay, by a policy which
I have ever ventured to doubt the wiſdom of,
we had very conſiderable armies, beyond the

ability

ability of either Government to fupport. But ftill the military force was moft refpectable; if fufficient pains had not been taken to fecure the due payment of the fums which the Carnatic and Tanjore were to advance each year, the error is *yours*.

. England had fully recovered its confequence amongft the nations of Europe, and the King's India Minifters and Parliament, wifely gave that full *fupport* and *confidence* to Lord Cornwallis, which they *denied* to Mr. Haftings.

Under all thefe favourable circumftances a war was determined upon. The Marattas and the Nizam, who were *friends* to Hyder Ally Cawn in the laft war, were enemies to Tippoo Sultaun in this.

The

The French who fent, in the courfe of the laft war, feventeen fail of the line with frigates, five thoufand land forces, and feven millions fterling to India, (though part of the force and money was interrupted in its way out) had not a man upon the continent in this war, who had even a wifh to venture beyond the walls of Pondicherry ; fo torn and divided were they by inteftine commotions.

With all thefe favourable circumftances, General Medows, foon after he came to Madras, and before an army was affembled, foretold the *abfolute neceffity* of feizing the Government of the Carnatic.

Suppofe *Mr. Haftings* had expreffed fuch fentiments, what would you, and Mr. Pitt, and the Managers, have faid *to him?* Again, let me guard myfelf from the fufpicion of intending

tending a reflection upon General Medows ;
it is your approval of *those sentiments*, in op-
position to *your recorded principles*, that strikes
me with astonishment.

I understand from Captain Broome, in his
excellent Elucidation, that had Mr. Hastings
justified his acts on the plea of *necessity*, not a
word would have been said against him by
you ; but that he had urged *false motives*
for violent measures.

Take it upon this ground, though I believe the reverse is clear to the whole world,
and then *I will say*, that provided you have
written to Madras in the *following terms*,
you are in this instance perfectly consistent :

    " We have received, and read with the
" utmost attention, all your late proceedings

R   " rela-

" relative to the Nabob of Arcot and the Ra-
" jah of Tanjore; we have also examined,
" with the strictest accuracy, every clause
" in the treaties concluded with those
" Princes, *by our orders*, and to which we
" have given our *warmest approbation*. We
" shall now proceed to give you our senti-
" ments and our directions for your future
" guidance."

" Knowing, as you well did, the very se-
" vere distresses which our several Govern-
" ments laboured under in the late war,
" from a want of pecuniary supplies, we are
" not surprized that the amount of the ar-
" rears, which were due to you from the
" Carnatic and Tanjore, when war was in-
" evitable, became a subject of your most
" serious consideration. We do not at all
" differ with you in opinion, upon the con-
" sequence

" fequence it was to our interefts, to conci-
" liate the polygars and tributaries of the
" Carnatic before the war commenced, and
" during its continuance; for if it was pro-
" longed beyond one campaign, there was
" every reafon to believe that Tippoo would
" make an incurfion into the Carnatic, as
" he actually did in December 1790."

" It is impoffible, therefore, for us to with-
" hold our approbation from you, becaufe
" every thing that you have done, appears
" to proceed from a regard to our interefts."

" But *we* are placed in fo very different a
" fituation, that there are fome cafes in
" which *we* are not at liberty to exercife our
" own difcretion. The *legiflature* has ftrict-
" ly enjoined a facred obfervance of treaties,
" and we have, on a former occafion, tranf-

R 2   " mitted

" mitted certain *refolutions* moved in Parlia-
" ment, in which an *inviolable regard to the*
" *faith of treàties* is moſt particularly recom-
" mended."

" The only point left, therefore, for our
" conſideration is, whether by the *letter*
" or *the ſpirit* of the treaties concluded by
" Sir Archibald Campbell, you could, under
" any circumſtances ſhort of a voluntary
" ſurrender of their dominions, by the Na-
" bob and the Rajah, have aſſumed the Go-
" vernment of the Carnatic and Tanjore ?"

" We are compelled to declare, that the
" very caſe which gave riſe to your ſeizure
" of the countries, is moſt expreſſly provi-
" ded for, and you are *precluded*, in poſitive
" terms, by the treaties, from taking the
" countries."

" If

" If by any neglect of the late adminiſtra-
" tion, meaſures were not adopted for reco-
" vering the balance that was due when our
" preſent Governor arrived, we do not ſee
" how the Nabob and the Rajah are to be
" made reſponſible *in the manner that you
" have made them reſponſible.*"

" In the even of failure on peace you had
" *a right* to collect the rents from the Na-
" bob Aumils; in war you had a right to
" ſend inſpectors; and Sir Archibald Camp-
" bell actually bound the Britiſh nation to
" proceed *no farther* on any contingency
" *whatever.*"

" Indeed your own ſtatement of the
" caſe renders argument unneceſſary. You
" thought the treaties inefficient, and fairly
" con-

" conceived that you had, therefore, a right
" to violate them."

" We are exceedingly forry to find, that
" fuch are *your fentiments* of treaties which
" were *originally* planned *by us*, and which
" Sir Archibald Campbell concluded *entirely*
" *to our fatisfaction*. But the queſtion for
" us to confider is, not whether the treaties
" are or are not inefficient, but whether
" the *British faith* was pledged for the obfer-
" vance of them ? there muſt be an end of
" all confidence in treaties in India, if a par-
" ty conceiving it has made an inefficient
" engagement ſhall be at liberty to break it,
" whenever it fuits his conveniency."

" It is incumbent *upon us* to recollect that
" Mr. Haſtings has been under a profecution
" for five years in the name of all the peo-
" ple

" ple of Great Britain, and the leading fea-
" ture of his Impeachment was, a breach of
" faith, not to an ally of the Company, but
" to the *mother* and *subject* of an ally. No
" doubt can be entertained but that the *origi-*
" *nal engagement* formed with her, to which
" the Company was *the guarantee,* was in
" the higheft degree *impolitic.* To allow the
" mother of the Nabob of Oude to retain
" in her poffeffion for fix years, at leaft one,
" and probably more than two millions fter-
" ling, to command a military force and to
" exercife an *independent authority* in her
" fon's dominions, was dangerous and im-
" proper, but the *national faith* was pledged
" for her *fecurity,* and Mr. Haftings was
" impeached on a charge of having violated
" it."

" We

" We voted for that Impeachment *in ano-*
" *ther character*, but as Minifters, we ought
" not to *abandon* all the *principles* that we
" have profeffed, as Members of a Britifh
" fenate."

" At the fame time that we exculpate *you*
" from all blame, in having feized the go-
" vernment of the Carnatic and Tanjore,
" contrary to a folemn treaty, we fhould
" deem ourfelves deeply criminal indeed,
" if we did not order you, as we now moft
" peremptorily do, *inftantly* to reftore the
" Carnatic to the Nabob, and Tanjore to
" the Rajah."

" We farther direct that you enforce the
" ftipulated payments from each, by every
" mode that you can, *confiftently* with the

2   " *letter*

" *letter* and *spirit* of Sir A. Campbell's *trea-*
" *ties*, but that you go no *farther*."

Orders of this nature would be perfectly
confonant to your *profeffions*.

ASIATICUS.

Jan. 25, 1792.

LETTER X.

SIR,

THAT the inconfiftencies which I have laid to your charge, may not be loft in the length and multiplicity of the arguments through which they are diffufed, I will briefly fum up the fubftance of them, in diftinct articles.

1ft. That you moved and carried a Refolution in Parliament, that the ftoppage of the tribute of the Emperor Shaw Allum was contrary to *policy* and *good faith*; and that fuch wife and practicable meafures fhould be adopted *in future*, as might redeem *the national honour*. Yet though this refolution paffed in

1782,

1782, and you have yourself been intrufted with the means of carrying it into execution, and have been in effect the acting Minifter for the affairs in India, from 1784, you have neither caufed the tribute to be *reftored*, nor taken *any one meafure*, either to *redeem*, or *palliate* the lofs of the *national* honour.

2d. You have voted *as a Member of Parliament*, that Mr. Haftings made demands of money upon Cheyt Sing, for three fucceffive years, *contrary to treaty*, and that he *unjuftly* and *tyrannically* expelled him from *his dominions*; yet though pofitively enjoined by law, to *reftore* every Rajah and Zemindar who had been *unjuftly* difpoffeffed, you have not reftored Cheyt Sing; on the contrary, you have taken credit *annually* for an additional revenue of two hundred thoufand pounds a year, *obtained by his expulfion*. You cannot

fay

say that you wait the result of Mr. Haftings's
impeachment, because you became the India
Minifter in *Auguft* 1784, and *ought* to have
fent orders *forthwith*, that is, in the *firft year*
of your minifterial duty, for his reftoration.
His expulfion was not ftated to be *criminal* by
the Commons, until June 1786, nearly *two
years* after you had been the Minifter of
India.

3d. You voted on the 9th of May 1787,
that Bengal was ruined and depopulated, her
Revenues *diminifhed*, and her inhabitants *deftroyed*, with an infinite variety of circumftances expreffive of mifery, wretchednefs,
and oppreffion. But on the 7th, two days
only *preceding*, you had proved the *increafe*
of the revenues, by the *evidence of figures*.
You unequivocally declared that Bengal was
the beft governed country in India, and that

the

the ftate of our empire in India, as compared to *this country*, was as *light*, oppofed to *dark-nefs*. Such a remark could only apply to Bengal, in other words *to Mr. Haftings*, for Madras and Bombay did not pay *their own charges, by half a million a year at the leaft.*

4th. You repeated the fame fentiments each year, from 1787 to this day, and you *patiently* heard the Managers in Weftminfter-hall, who unequivocally in each year proclaimed *the ruin of Bengal*, through the mal-adminiftration of Mr. Haftings.

5th. You *approved*, in four feveral letters to Bengal, of certain arrangements formed by Mr. Haftings in Qude, and you ordered that they fhould be *invariably adhered to.* As a Member of Parliament, you voted that the

delega-

delegation, under which he formed thofe ar-rangements was *illegal*; you *condemned* the *arrangements*, and voted that Mr. Haftings was guilty of high crimes and mifdemeanors for having formed them.

6th. In 1782, you moved a refolution in Parliament, that to feize the government and revenues of Tanjore, would be a breach of faith, and *oppreffive* and *ruinous* to the *country*; and if fo feized, it was the duty of the Directors to order them *to be forthwith re-ftored* to the Rajah. In 1790, the revenues and government were feized, *in avowed breach of treaty*. In 1791, you *completely* and *entirely approve* this tranfaction, and do *not* order them to be forthwith *reftored*, or to be reftored at all, though the Rajah is even *intemperate* in his complaints of the injuftice of the Britifh Government.

7th.

7th. In 1782, you recorded it as a *fixed, unalterable principle*, that treaties fhould be *inviolably preferved.* The law ftates the fame principles. In 1786, you fent *orders* to Sir Archibald Campbell to conclude two treaties, one with the Nabob, and the other with the Rajah of Tanjore. Sir Archibald obeys your orders ; you tranfmit to him *your warmeft approbation,* for the *manner* in which he carried *your orders* into execution. In 1790, the Government of Madras break thefe treaties, and in 1791, you *approve* of their conduct.

8th. You have prohibited and condemned all wars for conqueft and extent of dominion, in India ; yet you approve of the prefent war, which has for its object *conqueft*, and extent of dominion.

9th.

9th. In the year 1784, you tranfmit your thanks to Mr. Haftings. (For the *law* makes every act of the Directors *yours*, fince it is nugatory until it has received your approbation.) In the year 1785, you tranfmit an acknowledgement of his *long, faithful, and able fervices.* In the year 1787, you *condemn* as *criminal,* all the acts of his adminiftration, *civil,* military, *political,* and *finan-cial.*

I have now but a few obfervations to add, and fhall then take my leave.

In the courfe of thefe Letters I have been very careful to apply the conftruction, which I have put upon your meafures, to yourfelf alone, or to Mr. Pitt, acting in concert with you. I include none elfe in the charge, whether of inconfiftency, injuftice, or impolicy.

2   The

The quality of human actions is seldom intrinsecally, but always relatively, good or evil. Of the guilt which I have imputed to you, some may be culpable in a venial degree; others wholly innocent, although both may have been participators, or even perpetrators of the acts from which it is inferred. Nay, I will go yet farther, and say, that it may so happen from a different relation of the same act and of its agents, that it shall be criminal in one, and yet meritorious in another.

For instance: all the acts which are mentioned in the preceding articles and which concern Mr. Hastings, are meritorious, as they respect him, because he thought them so: but they are highly criminal in Mr. Dundas, because he has joined *in a solemn condemnation of them*; and yet has suffered the continuance of some, *having the power to*

· T   *revoke*

revoke them; and has himſelf iſſued orders *for the confirmation of the reſt.*

The preſent war in India may be, as I think I have proved, warranted by ſtrict juſtice, and reconcileable to ſound policy; and ſo far it reflects credit on Lord Cornwallis who engaged in it. But the ground on which it is juſtifiable *abroad*, will not avail Mr. Dundas at home, who has adopted the reſponſibility of it, in direct contradiction to a law of of his own formation, which expreſſly condemns all ſchemes of conqueſt and extent of dominion ; and yet theſe are the declared objects of the war.

But for the firſt preparatory operation of the war, namely, the ſeizure of the Carnatic, I do not find myſelf ſo well qualified to decide on the relative quality of this tranſaction,

tion, as of the others in which you bear, as in this, a principal share. On your part of it I have no doubt what judgement to pafs. The treaty with the Nabob was formed under your order requiring it. You approved it and ratified it: yet in three years afterwards you approved and ratified the violation of it, on precifely the fame ground for which the treaty itfelf had exprefsly provided a remedy in the very article of it which was violated. No plea can excufe, no fophiftry can cover the enormity of fuch a tranfaction. Far different is the cafe of the gentlemen of Madras in relation to it. They had no fhare in the formation of the treaty, nor does it appear that they had any in the ratification of it: on the contrary, the firft notice that we find them take of it, is a declaration of its utter *inefficiency*, *inutility*, and a proteft againft the obfervance it, on the plea that the war

T 2   could

could not be maintained, nor the Carnatic defended, *without an abfolute departure from it.* I do not juftify the plea : but certainly there is a wide difference between their breach of a treaty, in which they had no other concern, and which they thought of dangerous tendency to their interefts, of which they had charge, and your breach of a treaty made under your own exprefs authority, and ratified by your own fanction.

What defence Lord Cornwallis may fet up for the authority which he gave upon this occafion, I will not take upon me to fuggeft. I am not his advocate, nor would it become me to offer in his juftification reafons which he may difclaim, or to afcribe to him motives which he alone can know. But as I think it incumbent upon me to declare, that I mean not by any thing that I have written

to

to caft the leaft reproach or infinuation upon his Lordfhip ; fo I may with propriety affign my own reafons for making this diftinction,

From the records of this affair, which have been publifhed, it appears that Lord Corn-wallis has adopted the plea cf the Governor and Council of Fort St. George, but fo fee-bly as to indicate a ftrong reluctance to yield to it, and rather the appearance of a defire to be convinced, than an actual conviction of its validity. Poffibly, taking his judgement of the neceffity from thofe who had the beft means of forming it, he did believe the cir-cumftances to be as they were ftated to him; although the contrary may be inferred from his elufiye reply to their firft requifition of his authority, to take by force the manage-ment of the Government of the Carnatic ; and when preffed to it in terms which left

him

him no other alternative, but to relinquifh the war already declared, or to profecute it without any hope of affiftance from the re- fources of the Carnatic, he then, it is true, did yield his affent, but repeated, in a very earneft manner, the recommendation of his former letter, that they would ftill endeavour to obtain their claim by folicitation, rather than poffefs themfelves of it by force. If in this cafe he gave way to a ftrong political neceffity, let it be remembered that the war was wholly of his direction. The Members who were then of the Council at Madras, had no concern whatever in the formation of it, nor in the firft fteps which led to it ; and General Medows, the Governor of Madras, on whom the conduct of the war depended, was but newly arrived there. The whole refponfibility of the war, therefore, to this time, refted on Lord Cornwallis ; and if it

2   failed

failed of fuccefs, from the want of thofe means which they had ftated to him to be indifpenfably neceffary, the whole blame of it would, by his refufal to avail himfelf of them, fall on him alone, befides the chance of other confequences infinitely worfe than any that could affect him as an individual. Had he been himfelf upon the fpot, he might have tried the effect of that conciliation which he recommended.. No occafion exifted at that time which could have juftified him in quitting the feat and fcene of his own Government, to go to Madras. He embarked by himfelf in a hazardous plan, for the execution of which, he depended abfolutely on the agency of others; and they had in a manner prefcribed to him the terms on which they could or would undertake it. In a word, whoever will give himfelf the trouble to review the fituation of

Lord

Lord Cornwallis in this conjuncture, and candidly weigh all the confequences of it in any decifion which he could have formed upon it, will be convinced that cafes may occur in the conduct of great affairs, (and that this was one of them) in which an option may be prefented, not only of political difficulties to be furmounted, but of moral evils to be reconciled to the principle of political duty.

ASIATICUS.

26th Jan. 1792.

THE END.